MY ADVENTURES

WITH

Disney FAIRIES

This book was especially written for
Darcy Cowie
with love from
Nana Lang

Visit www.disneyfairies.com

© 2007 Disney Enterprises, Inc.
By Wendy Elks and Kate Andresen
ISBN 1 875676 22 8

If you head toward the second star on your right and fly straight on till morning you'll come to Never Land where fairies live and magic is as common as laughter. It's called Never Land, because everyone that lives there never grows old.

You may have heard of Peter Pan, and his tiny fairy-friend, Tinker Bell. Tink lives in a place called Pixie Hollow, with lots of other fairies and sparrow men.

They play games, like fairy tag, which are exciting and fun. But they work hard, too. There are many important jobs to do in Pixie Hollow and all the fairies have different talents to ensure everything runs smoothly.

Darcy believes in fairies. And it happened that once, when Darcy was playing at the seaside with Amelie, Esme and Jeanette, a strange and magical thing happened.

They were sitting on the sand, making necklaces out of pretty shells and shiny seed pods, and tiny pieces of green and pink seaweed that looked just like lace. The necklaces looked beautiful, and Darcy, Amelie, Esme and Jeanette clapped with joy.

It was a warm and sunny day and the sky was very blue. Sunlight sparkled on the water, so brightly that it shone like glitter in Darcy's eyes.

Darcy rubbed her eyes, but the shimmering light got stronger. All of a sudden she was floating... flying... straight towards Never Land!

Never Land is a magical island. It can ride atop waves and move in any direction it likes. Beautiful mermaids swim in the sparkling blue lagoon nearby. Captain Hook lives on his ship, the *Jolly Roger*, in Pirate Cove, and the Lost Boys live in their underground home. There's even a dragon, called Kyto who is imprisoned in a cave in Torth mountain.

Pixie Hollow is the secret heart of Never Land. A grand old maple tree grows there.

Darcy couldn't believe that she was heading for Never Land. She was a bit frightened, but also very excited. The sparkling sea lay far below and it looked very deep. Darcy almost wanted to dive in to see if there really were mermaids living there!

Soon she was flying low over lush green forest, and she saw several small, glowing lights coming towards her. When she got closer, she realised that they were fairies!

'Welcome to Never Land, Darcy,' said a pretty blonde fairy, dressed in green. It was Tinker Bell!

Darcy was overjoyed but also a little confused. Tink explained that, in recognition of Darcy's unconditional belief in fairies, she had been chosen to visit Never Land for a day!

There were two other fairies with Tink. Fira, or Moth, as Tink called her, was a light-talent fairy. Her glow could single-handedly light the entire Home Tree.

The other member of the welcoming committee was Rani, who looked very gracious sitting on the back of Brother Dove. Rani is the only fairy without wings.

'Fly with you,' she said giving the Never fairy greeting, then blew her nose on a leafkerchief. Rani wasn't crying, she was just full of water, as usual.

Down, down, down they flew, towards Pixie Hollow.

When they landed they found themselves caught up in a game of fairy tag. Water-talent fairies were hurling balls of water at the other fairies and sparrow men and there were shouts of 'Choose you' echoing throughout the meadow.

Suddenly, a fairy dressed in leaf-green, with light brown hair and green boots, galloped by on a chipmunk.

'Hey, Beck!' Tink called to her. 'Meet Darcy.'

'Fly with you, Darcy,' Beck said, welcoming her. She patted the chipmunk and they sped off.

'Come on, let's go on a tour of Pixie Hollow,' said Tink. 'We'll dress you as a fairy, and tonight there'll be a special celebration where all the fairies will put on a show for you. You'll even get to meet Mother Dove!'

Mother Dove is the spiritual leader of the Never fairies and she watches over them with unconditional love and affection. In turn, the fairies look to her for guidance and comfort.

'Before we do anything, though, we need to find Terence,'
Tink said. 'You're almost our size, Darcy, but you're still a
lot heavier than us fairies. You'll need an extra dose of fairy
dust to make you fly.'

Tink whistled, and a sparrow man flew over. Terence was
a dust-talent sparrow man. He was in charge of measuring
and distributing the fairy dust that enabled fairies to fly, and
do their magic.

Terence had sparkling blue eyes. In fact he sparkled all over, because he carried and ladled out fairy dust all day long. When he'd finished spreading the fairy dust, they flew off.

Up ahead was a towering old maple, the Home Tree. Nestled amongst its massive branches, and many boughs, lay the tiny rooms and workshops of the fairies. Each room had been uniquely decorated according to the fairies' talent and personality.

Tink introduced Darcy to Prilla, a recent arrival. Prilla is Never Land's first and only mainland-visiting clapping-talent fairy—she can transport herself to the mainland where she can interact with Clumsy children and, if necessary, persuade them to clap to save a fairy. Prilla's talent is very important, for by keeping up children's belief in fairies, she can, in turn, save many a fairy's life.

'Amelie, Esme and Jeanette won't believe me when I tell them where I've been today. I wonder where they are now?' Darcy asked Prilla.

'Why don't we go and see?' replied Prilla as she took Darcy's hand and transported her back to the mainland. They found Amelie, Esme and Jeanette at Darcy's home at Invercowie House, in Stonehaven. They were reading aloud from their favourite book 'Peter and Wendy'.

Darcy smiled and clapped her hands and Prilla whisked her back to Never Land where Tink was waiting to greet her.

Tink was a pots-and-pans fairy. She loved to make broken things whole again. Hammering shiny tin and copper went with her fiery nature.

Tink spent most of her time in her workshop. It had been made from an old kettle she'd found and cleaned and polished inside and out. She'd turned the spout upside down to make a door awning and punched out openings for windows and doors. It had a parquet floor and shiny steel domed walls and ceiling.

Tink was clever, and brave. Once she'd rescued Peter Pan from a shark by sprinkling him with fairy dust, so he could fly. He and Tink had become best friends.

She gazed around her workshop, looking for something special to give to Darcy.

'When is your birthday, Darcy?' Tink asked.

'The twenty-first of January,' replied Darcy.

In a trice, Tink had engraved Darcy's name and the twenty-first of January on a shiny gold medallion. She strung it on a golden chain and hung it around Darcy's neck.

'There—something to remember me by, when you go home,' she said.

Darcy was thrilled. 'Oh, Tink, how could I ever forget *you*,' she said.

'Let's go! It's time to meet some of the other fairies,' said Tink as they flew towards the next room that had been cleverly decorated with an old artist's palette and paint brushes. A paint brush had even been attached to the front door to serve as a door handle! This obviously belonged to Bess, an art-talent fairy.

Bess was in her garden painting a picture of a beautiful bunch of flowers that Lily, a garden-talent fairy had given her. Bess had splashes of red, green and pink paint all over her face and clothing. The inside of her room was even more spectacular with magnificently carved sculptures and works of art. Displayed above Bess's bed was a serene portrait of Mother Dove.

Bess was able to see the beauty in everything, and make each thing even more beautiful.

'You have lovely hair,' Bess told Darcy as they sat with Tink and Rani on Bess's bed. 'But it would look even nicer with some tiny braids and flowers.'

'Good idea,' Tink said. 'Darcy's birth flower is the carnation. They'll look great, Bess. She will look beautiful for the celebration tonight.'

Soon Darcy was having her hair braided by a fairy!

While they chatted and laughed, Darcy thought she heard a scuffle outside the window. She felt that someone was out there, watching her—someone who didn't want to be seen.

Who, or what, was it? This was Never Land, after all. Perhaps it was Kyto, the dragon!

They left Bess's room and called in at Rani's room because she needed to pick up more leafkerchiefs. Rani's room was at the top of a spiral staircase.

Rani is a water-talent fairy who loves anything that has to do with water. Her beautiful room is made out of an unusually large seashell that washed up on the beach long ago. Her room is decorated with delicate seaweed curtains and shiny shells and her bed is made out of driftwood. The scalloped rim of her patio makes a perfect perch for Brother Dove who has been her wings since she lost her own.

In contrast to the peaceful surroundings, Rani is a bundle of energy. She can't keep still for long, and she has a habit of finishing people's sentences, because she can't wait for them to do it. But she is so happy and enthusiastic about everything, she is a joy to be around.

While Rani was getting her leafkerchiefs there was another scuffle outside the window. And was that a... giggle? In that case, whoever was out there most likely wasn't a dragon.

As they flew from Rani's room to Beck's, a streak of red slipped from bush to bush. Somebody—or some *thing*—was following them!

Beck was at home, making arrangements for the celebration with Mother Dove. Beck and her fellow animal-talent fairies were putting on a show that night. She was briefing her good friend Twitter, the hummingbird, on the choreography for their aerial display.

Beck loaned Darcy her favourite silk-and-spider web wrap to wear to the dinner. It was so light and delicate, and yet wonderfully warm and cosy.

Darcy heard a rustle outside Beck's door. She was growing nervous. What if it was Captain Hook, or one of the nasty pirates?

She looked towards the door. 'I thought I—'

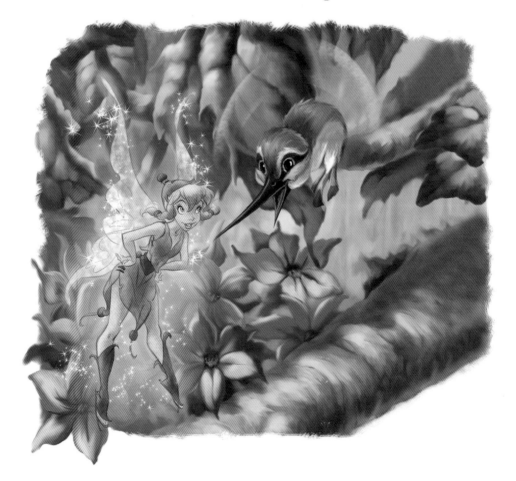

'—heard something,' finished Rani, looking puzzled.

Suddenly there were peels of laughter. A fairy with auburn curls cart-wheeled into Beck's living room.

'Prilla, you trickster!' Tink cried.

Prilla laughed, and did another cart-wheel.

Since Prilla is the only member of her talent, the other fairies make her feel welcome and loved by making her an honorary member of each of their own talents.

'Where are we going now?' Prilla asked excitedly.

'*We're* going on a tour of Never Land,' answered Tink. 'But aren't *you* meant to be helping the baking-talent fairies, Prilla?'

'Well, I was,' said Prilla. 'But, I burnt the pumpkin muffins. Then I gave the raisins to the birds, because I thought they were old, wrinkled blueberries. Then I beat the cream too much and it turned into butter. But at least we have lots of butter, now. When I started eating the strawberry angel food cupcakes, Dulcie suggested it was time for me to leave. So, here I am.'

Tink shrugged. 'Okay, you'd better come with us then. We've only got half an hour before the party starts to show Darcy the whole of Never Land. Let's go!'

The little group headed north. They flew over the rolling hills and valleys of Never Land. In the middle of the island the dark mountains soared, where Kyto the dragon lived. 'We don't go there,' Tink called over her shoulder.

She made for the coast, and the lagoon where the mermaids played. Their laughter could be heard floating up from the turquoise water. Further on in a bay of dark, deep water, a sailing ship lay at anchor. A tiny Captain Hook could be seen, pacing the deck. Rani pointed out the entrance to the underground home of the Lost Boys.

All too soon it was time to go back and get ready for the party. Back in Pixie Hollow at the fairy circle, Darcy saw light-talent fairies herding fireflies into position, and celebration-setup-talent fairies arranging tables and chairs. Golden sunlight was slanting through the trees. It was going to be a beautiful evening on Never Land.

Queen Clarion's gazebo was always decorated with flowers, but this afternoon it looked magnificent. Masses of spider webs had been strung from the Home Tree to the gazebo, and hung with firefly lanterns. Darcy had never seen such a spectacle!

'Come on, Darcy, it's time to find you an outfit for tonight,' said Rani smiling.

They visited the style-talent fairies, where they tried on the most gorgeous fairy clothes imaginable and selected beautiful, shining jewels and accessories.

When their outfits had been selected, there was time to visit the tearoom for a quick peppermint tea accompanied by the most delicious fig-chocolate cake.

The sky was a deepening blue and the clouds tinged with orange and pink.

'I have to go and start the fountain,' Rani said, popping the last of her cake into her mouth.

'Okay,' Tink said. 'We'll go to Prilla's to get dressed. There's more room at her place.'

Off they went, through balmy air full of delicious scents and the sounds of the band tuning their instruments.

At Prilla's, Darcy and the two fairies helped each other to get ready. Prilla couldn't decide what kind of flower petals to wear in her hair.

'The carnations,' suggested Darcy. 'They'll go perfectly with your dress.' Tink didn't really care much for dressing up. She liked practical clothes, that didn't get in the way of tinkering. But tonight she made an effort and put on her prettiest dress.

'You look beautiful, Tink,' exclaimed Darcy. Then she remembered the shell necklace she'd been making at the beach, before this magical adventure began. She took it out of her pocket and put it round Tink's neck. It was perfect, and Tink loved it. 'It's yours to keep,' said Darcy.

They were all dressed up and it was time to go to the dance. The sky was a deep, dark blue, with just a tinge of gold on the horizon. Overhead, huge stars were shining. There were fireflies everywhere, so it wasn't dark.

From the leafy boughs of the Home Tree, shimmering fairies in delicate outfits made of petals and lace were heading for the dance. Down in the clearing, the tables, covered in white and decorated with flowers, were filling with guests.

Most of the fairies sat with their talent-groups, but a special table had been reserved for the special guest. Tink headed for this table. Already seated there were Rani, Bess, Beck, Terence, and Prilla.

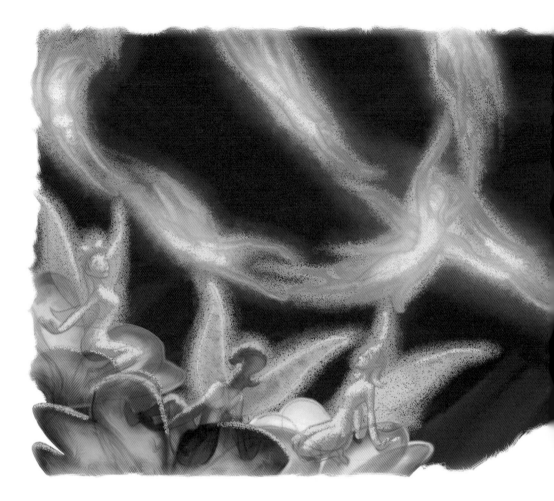

Darcy sat at the table. She was happy and excited, but
nervous too. Rani squeezed her hand, and Beck smiled
shyly. Prilla was hugging herself. Darcy realised the fairies
were feeling the same as she was. It was a special occasion
for all of them.

Soon a great feast was in progress. Darcy forgot to be
nervous as she talked and laughed with her new friends, and
nibbled delicious morsels of fairy food.

By now it was dark, and the moon had risen. Tiny lights
twinkled everywhere. Suddenly there was a flash. Fira, the
light-talent fairy, appeared in a burst of fire-works.

Fira and the light-talent fairies put on a dazzling show
that left everyone gasping. Next, Rani and the other water-
talents created spectacular fountain displays.

Then the animal-talent fairies, led by Beck, performed
aerial acrobatics on Twitter and the hummingbird family!
Swooping and diving above the tables, drenched in fairy
dust, they thrilled and enchanted the audience.

'That was great,' Prilla said afterwards, her pink cheeks
glowing with excitement. 'But I hope dessert is next.'

But Prilla would have to wait for dessert. The band
struck a stirring tune, and hundreds of fireflies moved to
the gazebo. A hush fell over the tables. Queen Clarion was
about to appear.

Queen Clarion's gazebo was set high on a rock, overlooking the fairy kingdom. A regal, elegant figure, shimmering with pixie dust, appeared. Darcy gasped as the fairy Queen looked straight at her. 'Welcome to Never Land, Darcy,' Queen Clarion said.

Darcy felt so special! Everyone applauded, and her fairy friends beamed at her. Tink and Prilla clapped the loudest, and Rani had to wipe tears from her eyes. They were proud of Darcy!

'It's very important that Clumsies keep believing in fairies,' Queen Clarion said. 'Every time a child or adult stops believing, a fairy dies. This is a very serious matter.'

Then Queen Clarion smiled. 'But tonight is a happy occasion. Children around the world mostly *do* believe in fairies, so the fairy realm of Never Land will keep growing. Prilla, and our other recent arrivals are proof of that.'

Smiling, Prilla's glow turned red as her hair.

'Mother Dove would like to meet our special guest,' Queen Clarion continued. 'Tink... Beck... Rani... would you be escorts, please.'

Tink and Beck took Darcy's hands, and gently pulled her from her chair. With Rani and Brother Dove leading the way, they rose above the tables, and the twinkling lights.

Not far away, nestled in a hawthorn bush, was Mother Dove's nest. The magical bird looked big to Darcy who was as small as the fairies around her. Her eyes were gentle and kind, and she cooed softly in welcome.

Mother Dove picked up something shiny with her beak, and offered it to Darcy. It was a garnet, her birthstone. As Darcy took the gift, she saw the pixie glow fading from her hands and she realised that this unforgettable night would soon end and she would have to go home.

But it wasn't over yet. Back at the fairy circle, the dance was in full swing and all the fairies were dancing in the glow of fireflies. As it was a Never dance, it just might go on forever!

The joyful sounds of music and laughter echoed across Pixie Hollow. Darcy was beginning to feel sleepy and Tink realised that it was time for her to go. All the fairies gathered around and whispered softly 'Fly again soon, Darcy, and keep on believing.' Prilla took Darcy's hand and guided her back home to Stonehaven.

Far off, in the lagoon, the mermaids sang in reply and the Lost Boys danced and cheered. The whole of Never Land was celebrating the magic of fairies.

This personalised Disney Fairies book was especially created for Darcy Cowie of Invercowie House, Stonehaven, with love from Nana Lang.

If you ordered multiple books, they may be mailed separately — please allow a few days for differences in delivery times.

If Darcy loved starring in this personalised My Adventure Book then there are many more exciting stories in our collection.

Simply visit us at www.identitydirect.co.uk to create Darcy's next adventure!

Alternatively, you can contact us by by phone on 0845 450 5098.

Lots of exciting titles to collect!

8359 001076 0001 01 DS 0050

Order Ref #6131525

8 3 5 9 0 0 0 3 3 6 0 0 0 1 0 1